Little Bear Visits His Grandparents

By: Doug Renahan

Illustrated By: Jackie Johnston Ellett

ISBN: 0-89137-066-8

A note from the Author...

This book is dedicated to all the Grandparents who have spent countless hours telling make believe stories to their grandchildren. This dedication is also extended to those parents who have seen the gleam in their children's eyes when they were read the same stories.

Sincerely
"Daddy Doug"

Springtime had come to the forest.
All the snow was gone.
Flowers were blooming everywhere.

When Little Bear woke up on this sunny Saturday morning, he was very excited.

Now that the weather was warm, this was finally the day that he was going with his Mother and Daddy to visit his grandparents.

He had missed them so much during the winter when the snows were too deep to walk to their home.

He remembered the way Grandmother Bear always gave him cookies and milk for a treat.

He remembered the way Grandfather Bear always read him stories.

He wanted to show them the new teddy bear that he had gotten for Christmas.

He grabbed up his bear, jumped out of bed and ran downstairs to the kitchen.

While he was eating breakfast, he thought of Goldilocks and how much he would like for her to meet his grandparents.

He asked his mother if she would call and ask if Goldilocks could go along with them.

Mother Bear liked that idea so she called Goldilocks' mother to ask permission.

It was all right for Goldilocks to go with them.

She arrived at the Bear's house a little later, and they all set out through the woods together.

Grandmother and Grandfather Bear were very happy to see each one of them because it was lonely living in the deep woods by themselves.

Little Bear showed them his new teddy bear, then Grandmother invited them in for milk and cookies just as he hoped she would.

While the grown ups were talking,
Little Bear grabbed two cookies.

He and Goldilocks started to
explore the house while they ate
their cookies.

When they got to the living
room, Little Bear showed Goldilocks
an old piano that Grandmother
would let him play if he was careful.

Little Bear climbed on the piano stool which had a seat that went around and around.

After a while, he let Goldilocks spin on the stool.

She had as much fun as Little Bear did.

They took turns plunking down the piano keys and listening to the sounds they made.

Suddenly Little Bear stopped his playing.

He turned to Goldilocks and asked, "Would you like to go see the attic?"

"Oh, yes!" said Goldilocks.

Little Bear took her by the hand and they ran up to the attic door.

Little Bear opened the door.

There were all kinds of wonderful things in the attic.

There was an old picture album on a small table.

It was very dusty, but they were so curious to see the pictures inside that they opened it anyway.

The first picture they saw was of Grandmother and Grandfather Bear in their wedding clothes.

His grandparents looked **so** young that he couldn't believe it was them.

Grandmother Bear was very beautiful in her white dress.

Grandfather Bear looked handsome with his dark mustache.

As they turned the pages, they found more pictures of the bear family as it grew.

There was one of Little Bear's mother when she was a tiny cub.

There was another picutre of Mother Bear and her sister when they were about Little Bear's age.

After looking at a few more pictures, Little Bear noticed a large old trunk near them.

He went over and opened it slowly.

Inside the trunk were clothes that his grandparents had worn long ago.

Little Bear took out a black suit coat and a tall silk hat. He put them on. He found a pair of shiny black shoes and put them on too.

Goldilocks found a beautiful long dress, a hat with feathers, and some high-heeled shoes.

She put them on.

Goldilocks and Little Bear went parading around the attic trying to keep from tripping in the large shoes. They were laughing at the way it was hard to walk in the clothes.

Little Bear remembered that his grandfather had a mustache in his wedding picture.

He wanted one too.

Goldilocks was not sure that they should try to make a mustache, but Little Bear begged her to help him find something to make one.

They looked and looked until they finally found a bottle of black shoe polish.

Goldilocks painted a fine mustache above Little Bear's top lip.

He looked at himself in an old mirror that was leaning against a wall and felt very big.

Just then, Mother Bear came to the bottom of the attic stairs and called, "Lunch is ready!"

They quickly took off the dress-up clothes and carefully put them back where they belonged.

On the way down, Little Bear stopped at the washstand to take off the play mustache.

Goldilocks went on to the kitchen where a large wooden table was covered with good food.

They all sat down.

They began to wonder what was taking Little Bear so long.

Then Little Bear came into the kitchen with his head down and his paw over his mouth.

Daddy Bear asked, "Son, why do you have your paw over your mouth?"

Little Bear slowly took his paw away from his face.

There above his top lip was the mustache that he could not wash off.

He was so embarrassed that he was blushing through his fur.

Daddy Bear was so surprised to see a mustache on Little Bear that he started to laugh.

Everyone else began to laugh too. Now, Little Bear felt very small.

Before Little Bear could feel too badly, Grandfather Bear came over and hugged him.

He said to the others, "Don't laugh.

I remember some of the things that we did when we were young."

Mother Bear said, "You're right, Father."

Grandmother Bear said, "Well now, let's all eat lunch before the food gets cold."

Little Bear started to feel much better even though he could not wash off the play mustache.

After lunch, Grandfather Bear read a story to Goldilocks and Little Bear while Daddy Bear listened.

Mother Bear helped Grandmother Bear with the dishes.

After the dishes were done and the story was finished, it was time to leave for home.

They all hugged Grandfather and Grandmother Bear goodbye and started out for the Three Bears' house.

Every time Goldilocks saw Little Bear the rest of the Spring, with his shoe polish mustache slowly wearing off, she remembered the good time that she had at his grandparents' house.

Goldilocks remembered how much kindness and love they showed to her and Little Bear.

She also thought of how much she wanted to visit them again soon.